RUPERT
and the
Magic Hat

MARY TOURTEL

SBN 361 02957 8

SAMPSON LOW, MARSTON & CO., LTD.
London W.1.

Made and printed in Great Britain by Purnell and Sons Ltd.
Paulton (Somerset) and London

RUPERT AND THE MAGIC HAT

ONE morning Rupert wandered forth:
  He walked up to the moor
To enjoy the sunshine and fresh air
  As oft he had before.

All was so peaceful. Then the air
  Re-echoed to loud cries.
"What's that?" thought Rupert. "I must see,"
  And round the rocks he hies.

What sight is this? A little Gnome
  Being dragged along the ground
By a Monkey who shouts all the time:
  "Villain, at last you're found."

RUPERT AND THE
MAGIC HAT

"HANDS off, you Monkey," Rupert cried,
    "Let go that little man!"
The Monkey paused a moment as
    Rupert towards them ran.

As Little Bear drew nearer still
    The Monkey turned and fled.
"You'll be sorry that you interfered,
    Some day and soon," he said.

The Gnome rose quickly to his feet.
    "Thank you, my Little Bear.
You were just in time," said he, "to save
    Me from that ruffian there."

RUPERT AND THE
MAGIC HAT

"SAVE for your aid I had been lost.
  How can I you repay?"
Said the wily Gnome, "But come with me:
  My home's not far away."

So Rupert went. They'd not gone far
  When the Gnome said: "It is here,
Pray, enter." Rupert hesitates;
  It looks so dark and drear.

The Gnome said: "I will lead the way."
  So he goes on before,
Down some stone steps, and at the end
  He waits beside a door.

RUPERT AND THE MAGIC HAT

"COME in, for this is where I live
   By myself," explains the Gnome.
"Welcome to my poor house. Sit down
   And make yourself at home."

Quickly he spread a tablecloth,
   Brought cakes and currant wine,
And luscious fruits—grapes, peaches, pears.
   "And now," said he, "we'll dine."

"After dinner," said the little Gnome,
   "'Twill give to me great pleasure
To show you something I have got;
   It is my greatest treasure."

RUPERT AND THE
MAGIC HAT

TAKING Rupert to another room,
    Said the Gnome: "Now, what is that?"
Said Rupert: "Why, it looks to me
    A large size rolled-up hat."

"Exactly," said the Gnome, "but yet
    It's that and something more;
It's the Magic Hat that once belonged
    To Giant Blunderbore."

He took it up. "Come, follow me
    Outside. I'll show to you,"
Said he, "what this Most Wondrous Hat
    At my command will do."

RUPERT AND THE MAGIC HAT

THE Gnome put down the Hat when they
    Had reached the open moor,
Calling: "Open! Open! Quick Unfold!
    Magic Hat of Blunderbore!"

Ere Rupert scarce had time to think,
    The Hat unrolls and stands
Firm on its crown, obedient to
    The little Gnome's commands.

In leaped the Gnome. "Come for a ride
    Up in the air," said he;
"Unless you're frightened?" "No, I'll come,"
    Said Rupert instantly.

RUPERT AND THE MAGIC HAT

THE Hat rose gently in the air
  As though wafted on a breeze;
They float along, as in a dream,
  Above the fields and trees.

Rupert can see, below, the road
  That leads to his own home.
"How do you like it, Rupert, now?"
  Inquired the little Gnome.

"I like it very much indeed,"
  Said Rupert in reply.
"Well, hold on tight," the Gnome exclaimed;
  "We'll go higher in the sky."

RUPERT AND THE
MAGIC HAT

SOME time they floated high in air:
   Rupert below can see
The ocean. "Oh, where are we now?"
   He asks most anxiously.

"Wait," said the Gnome, "we'll soon see land,
   And then we will descend;
To see strange countries we will go
   Before our journey's end."

E'en as he spoke the land appeared,
   A fair isle lies below;
And soon a Palace comes in view
   As down and down they go.

RUPERT AND THE
MAGIC HAT

GENTLY the Hat comes down until
  It rests upon the ground.
Rupert climbs out. The Gnome before
  Had sprung out with a bound.

Said the Gnome: "A friend of mine doth live
  In the Palace yonder there;
I've a message I must give to him.
  Come with me, Little Bear."

Rupert looks round. A lovely place!
  Green lawns and flowers and trees;
With terraces; broad flights of steps.
  They go up one of these.

RUPERT AND THE MAGIC HAT

AT the top of that long flight of steps
A Gorgeous Person there
Greets the Gnome: "What's this you've brought
for us?
Surely, a little bear."

The Gnome snatched quickly off his cap,
And said he, bending low:
"I hope our Master will be pleased;
But one can never know."

RUPERT AND THE
MAGIC HAT

THE Gnome led Rupert to a room
    Said he, "Wait here for me
While I go to see my friend. Sit down;
    I'll be back speedily."

Rupert sat down; some long time passed:
    Still he knows he must wait.
"The Gnome's detained, perhaps," thinks he,
    "And that's why he is late."

Then a shadow on the window cast
    Draws his attention there;
He looks. Oh, what is that he sees
    Go sailing through the air?

RUPERT AND THE
MAGIC HAT

"STOP! stop! oh, stop! Don't leave me here!"
Cries Rupert to the Gnome.
"Oh, please, do fetch me! Do come back!
You said you'd take me home."

But all the time that cruel Gnome
Continued on his way.
He turned and grinned; then called, "Young Bear,
I wish you a Good Day."

RUPERT AND THE
MAGIC HAT

H E ran at once towards the door.
  Alas, he found it locked;
He kicked and hammered, loudly called;
  With hands he thumped and knocked.

Footsteps at last he hears approach,
  And in the lock a key
Is turned. He fearfully awaits,
  Wondering what he'll see.

It was a Monkey. Rupert said:
  "Oh, let me get away."
"Impossible," the Monkey said:
  "Once here, then you must stay."

RUPERT AND THE
MAGIC HAT

"YOU'RE to come with me," the Monkey said,
    "Straight to my Master now."
"Oh, no," cried Rupert, "let me go.
    Help me escape somehow."

"Help you to get away from here?"
    Said the Monkey. "Goodness me!
If you left this place, pray, tell me how
    You'd get across the sea?

"You're trapped, all through that wicked Gnome,
    As I was by him, too:
He brought me in his Magic Hat,
    The same way he brought you."

RUPERT AND THE
MAGIC HAT

JUST then they heard a roaring voice.
   "Oh, come," the Monkey cried.
"That's the Wild Boar; he's calling us."
   The two then rushed outside.

There, pompous, bristling, furious,
   They see the great Wild Boar.
"How dare you make my Master wait,"
   He shouts with angry roar.

RUPERT AND THE
MAGIC HAT

QUICKLY the Monkey takes him to
        A room; and seated there
Is a fierce old man in Eastern robes,
    Who glared at Little Bear.

"Is this the one the Gnome has brought
    For me to-day?" he said.
"Yes, sir," the Monkey answered, while
    Rupert stands there in dread.

"Ho! Ho!" he shouts to Rupert then.
    "We'll make some use of you.
You're not too young to help the Cook:
    For the kitchen you will do."

RUPERT AND THE MAGIC HAT

THEY reach the Kitchen. Rupert sees
    The Cook, a Chimpanzee,
Who's just about to taste the soup,
    When he looks round to see

Rupert and Jack (the Monkey's name).
    "Hullo, what have we here?"
Said the Cook. "Another little one,
    Like the rest, to disappear?"

RUPERT AND THE MAGIC HAT

THE Cook sets him, the Monkey, too,
    The knives and pots to clean.
Soon as he'd gone poor Rupert asked,
  "What did that old Cook mean?

"He seemed to think I'd disappear.
   What is this place, tell me?"
"I do not know," the Monkey said,
  "It's all a mystery.

"That fierce old man, our Master here,
   I dread. And just as you
I want to get away from here;
  But what are we to do?"

RUPERT AND THE
MAGIC HAT

"HI, there! you little bear," called Cook,
  "To the Kitchen Garden go;
I want some carrots now at once,
  You'll find nearby they grow."

Rupert took the basket. Miserable,
  The tears rolled down his face.
He fears what may become of him
  In that strange, sea-girt place.

"Through that cruel Gnome I'll ne'er see home,"
  Thinks Rupert in despair,
When he hears a voice: "Courage, my friend,
  I'll help you, Little Bear."

RUPERT AND THE MAGIC HAT

IT was a spotted Toad who spoke.
  "Ah, sad am I to see
You in the power of that old man.
  But, listen now," said she.

"Through his Secret Garden there's a way
  Will take you to the shore;
Watch for the Golden Butterfly.
  I cannot tell you more.

"Save that the venture's perilous
  And the Stone Horse is a clue."
So saying these strange words the Toad
  Hopped slowly out of view.

RUPERT AND THE
MAGIC HAT

RUPERT quickly fills his basket up
    With the carrots, for he's seen
Jack running up. "Cook waits," he calls.
    "Why, what a time you've been!"

"Oh," Rupert said, "I must tell you
    Of a way out that I've heard
For our escape. When we're alone
    I'll tell you every word."

RUPERT AND THE
MAGIC HAT

HE shared the Monkey's room that night.
    Eagerly Little Bear
Told him of what the Toad had said.
    "We daren't," Jack said, "go there.

"It's the Secret Garden. Once inside
    You're on enchanted ground,
So I've been told, and never more
    Is one seen again or found."

RUPERT AND THE MAGIC HAT

NEXT morning Little Bear was sent
    For fruit required that day
From the gardener for the old man's meals,
    Jack goes to show the way.

They pass a high, wrought-iron gate.
    "What's that?" asked Little Bear.
"That's the Secret Garden," Jack replied.
    "Quick! Come away from there."

"The one the Toad meant?" Rupert said.
    "Well, then, I'll climb that gate."
"Don't! Don't!" the Monkey said. "Oh, stop!
    Come back ere it's too late."

RUPERT AND THE MAGIC HAT

UNHEEDING, Rupert climbed the gate
  And soon he was inside.
"If you go I am coming, too!"
  Then Jack the Monkey cried.

"Oh," Rupert said, "I am so glad;
  I feared you'd stay behind:
I'm sure we will escape if we
  That Butterfly can find."

Then hand in hand they go along.
  Both fear to speak a word.
In that strange Garden not a sound
  But their footsteps can be heard.

RUPERT AND THE
MAGIC HAT

AT the bottom of a flight of steps the Monkey stopped in fear,
 And gripping Rupert's hand cried: "Look!" Two snakes
  were gliding near.
Rupert and Jack in fright spellbound with fixed gaze at them stare.
"Go back! Go back!" cried both the Snakes, "lest you our fate
  would share."

"We are two brothers, human once," said the Snakes, "and from
  our home
Were brought as slaves to that old man, betrayed thus by a
  Gnome.
Hard was our lot. One day we tried to escape, but caught were we
In this same Garden and by spells were changed to what you see."

RUPERT AND THE MAGIC HAT

Rupert and Jack hear them in dread and tremble for their fate
Should they be caught. But what's that sound? Someone unlocks
    the Gate.
The snakes then fled away from them with writhing, glissom glide,
While Jack and Rupert quickly run and in the bushes hide.

No sooner had they hid than down those steps they'd come before
Doth the old man stride, and at his side there stalks that big
    Wild Boar.
"We'll get them yet," the Wild Boar says. "That basket by the
    Gate
Tells me they're here, and, like the rest, they'll meet a well-
    earned fate."

RUPERT AND THE
MAGIC HAT

THEY watch them from their hiding-place
    Go searching everywhere—
Each bush and tree and all the paths:
    To move they do not dare.

When all seemed quiet, Jack said: "Quick,
    Let's run back to the Gate,
For if we're caught in here, you know
    Just what will be our fate."

"Oh, no," said Rupert, "now we're here
    We'll seek that Butterfly
Of which the Toad spoke yesterday:
    At least I mean to try."

RUPERT AND THE MAGIC HAT

So warily and on tip-toe from the bushes they crept out
For the Wild Boar and that old man may still be there about.
No sound they hear: they wander on. Jack gave a little cry,
And, pointing: "Look, there it is—the Golden Butterfly."

"Stop, stop, please Golden Butterfly! The Toad told me for you
I was to watch," cried Rupert, "and the Stone Horse was a clue
For our escape." The Butterfly flew down and settled near.
Said she: "It's true I can help you to get away from here."

RUPERT AND THE
MAGIC HAT

"THERE'S only one way of escape;
But you must first set free
A little bird shut in a cage
Ere I show it you!" said she.

"That Gnome among his victims brought
A Princess here one day,
A little girl. Like you," she said—
"She tried to get away;

"But caught she was by that old man,
Changed to a Nightingale;
And she must sing until he sleeps
Each day here without fail."

"E'EN now the old man's fast asleep,"
　　Said she; "follow my course;
I'll lead you to that bird and to
　　The Statue of the Horse.

"In the base of that stone Flying Horse
　　There is concealed a door
Worked by a spring which, open, shows
　　A passage to the shore.

"But first you must undo the cage
　　And set that poor bird free.
Beware you wake not that old man,
　　Or all is lost!" said she.

RUPERT AND THE
MAGIC HAT

DOWN grassy glades Rupert and Jack
    Follow that Butterfly.
She flits before them till at length
    The Stone Horse they draw nigh.

"Hist," said the Butterfly, "we're close!"
    (They hear the old man snore);
"Be careful, too, for often prowls
    Around that big Wild Boar.

"Wait here till I fly around to see
    In case he should be near."
But in a moment she returns
    To say that all is clear.

RUPERT AND THE
MAGIC HAT

FROM behind the Statue of the Horse
Then quietly they creep,
And there, full length upon a couch,
Is the old man fast asleep.

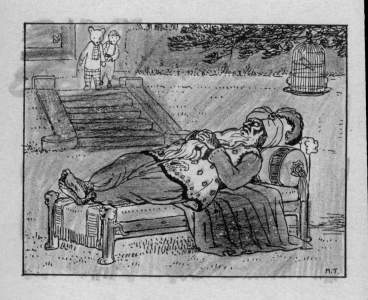

They see the bird there in a cage
Quite near the old man's head,
And one of them must set her free,
As the Butterfly had said.

RUPERT AND THE
MAGIC HAT

THE Butterfly tells them to haste;
　　No time must they lose now.
Rupert she bids undo the cage
　　Which hangs on yonder bough.

Jack has to climb the pedestal
　　And press a knob he'll see
In the Horse's hoof, and then a door
　　Will open quietly.

Jack climbs, keeping a wary eye
　　Lest the old man should wake,
While Rupert cautiously draws near
　　The little bird to take.

RUPERT AND THE MAGIC HAT

R UPERT safely reached the cage. The bird
Knew what he had come for.
He stands tip-toe and silently
Undoes the little door.

Oh! with what joy the bird flies off.
"Quick! Quick!" she seems to say,
As Rupert follows in her track
To where Jack points the way.

One anxious glance Jack cast behind:
But still the old man slept.
So through the open door, unseen,
Rupert and Jack both crept.

RUPERT AND THE
MAGIC HAT

IN their eager haste they both forgot
  To close the secret door
But scramble down a ladder, where
  A passage shows before,

Leading yet farther underground,
  They're frightened, all the three;
But through that darkness they must go
  From the old man to be free.

They grope along amid the gloom
  Some distance underground,
Till with joy they see the light of day—
  The way out they have found.

RUPERT AND THE
MAGIC HAT

THE sound of waves upon the shore tells them they're near
   the sea:
They walk down to a sandy bay and look round anxiously.
Just then the little bird called "Tweet!" as though to say,
   "Beware!"
Which made the two look up to see come sailing through the air

In his Magic Hat the Gnome—with him a passenger beside.
"Oh, oh," cried Jack, "look, look who's there! Come quickly, we
   must hide."
They crouched behind some rocks. By luck he had not looked
   below;
They watch him on his usual route to the old man's Garden go.

RUPERT AND THE
MAGIC HAT

MEANTIME, the old man had woke up;
   But what was his surprise?
The cage was empty, no bird there—
   He scarce could trust his eyes.

To make quite sure he looked again.
   "The bird has gone," he cried.
Then turning saw the Secret Door
   Itself was open wide.

RUPERT AND THE
MAGIC HAT

SOME one approached. He turns to see
   The Gnome come with the Boar.
"Odds bodikins! They've got away,"
   He shouts with angry roar.

"What's that?" the Gnome asks. He explains.
   "Don't worry, Master, soon
I'll bring them back," the Gnome replied—
   "This very afternoon.

"I've brought this little boy for you;
   He's the nicest I could get."
"Humph!" said the old man. "Well, be off;
   You've the others to find yet."

RUPERT AND THE MAGIC HAT

RUPERT and Jack climbed higher ground
   To gaze for any sail,
In hope some ship will rescue them
   If passing within hail.

Then suddenly the Magic Hat
   Approaching Jack espied.
"They've sent the Gnome to search for us;
   He's seen us here!" he cried.

RUPERT AND THE
MAGIC HAT

NO shelter's there where they can hide
    In that bare sandy place:
They hear the Gnome's loud chuckles as
    He gains on them apace.

They dash down hill; he's close behind.
    Rupert, in glancing back,
Falls headlong; tries to save himself,
    But only trips up Jack.

Ere they could rise the Hat descends,
    The Gnome jumps out with glee.
In his strong grip he has them both:
    "I've got you now!" cried he.

RUPERT AND THE
MAGIC HAT

BUT some one had been watching them:
  He had seen all that passed,
And, hurrying down, held up his hand
  And called: "Hi! Not so fast!"

They all looked up in wonderment,
  A man, fur-clad, to see.
"Now, tell me why you carry off
  These little ones?" asked he.

Said the Gnome: "It's none of your affair;
  Just kindly step aside."
Rupert and Jack imploring gazed:
  For help their looks implied.

RUPERT AND THE
MAGIC HAT

"A CIVIL answer I require;
    I see I am too polite,"
Said the stranger, picking up the Gnome,
    Who kicked and squealed in fright.

"How dare you treat me thus? I am
    Yanik, the Gnome, you know."
"Oh, ho," the stranger said, "and I
    Am Robinson Crusoe!"

RUPERT AND THE
MAGIC HAT

"OH, help us, please! Don't let the Gnome
          Get us again," they cry.
  "I'll see to that," he said. "Don't fear,
      He'll have no chance to try."

They tell him all about themselves,
    And about the little bird
And the old man in the Garden, too;
    'Twas a strange tale he heard.

Said Crusoe: "I must get my gun;
    I think 'twould be as well.
So come with me now, little ones,
    For nearby do I dwell."

RUPERT AND THE
MAGIC HAT

ERE they reach the cavern where he lives,
   The Gnome's tied to a tree
By Crusoe so he can't escape.
   "He's safe there now," said he.

Some bananas gathered fresh that day
   And milk he gives the two;
Then gets his gun. "Now, when you've done,"
   Said he, "we've work to do."

Jack's left to guard the Magic Hat,
   Rupert is Crusoe's guide.
He leads him to the opening,
   And points the way inside.

RUPERT AND THE
MAGIC HAT

ALONG the darksome way they grope
    Whence Rupert came before;
Ere long they reach the ladder steps.
    Still open stands the door.

Crusoe climbs through the opening.
    Said he: "Wait till I call.
'Twere best that you should stay behind,
    Lest harm should you befall."

RUPERT AND THE
MAGIC HAT

SOON face to face he came upon
    The old man—at his side
The Wild Boar, too. Quick as a flash
    "Hands up, both!" Crusoe cried.

Down on their knees they went, those two;
    Begged him their lives to spare.
"Have mercy," cried they, cowards both,
    With hands held high in air.

"I'll spare your lives," said Crusoe, "if
    At once you raise the spell
From all the children prisoned here—
    Your deeds I know full well."

RUPERT AND THE
MAGIC HAT

THE old man with his hands made signs,
   And, mumbling some strange word,
He gazed with fixed stare at the spot
   Where stood the little bird.

Crusoe looks round. What's this he sees?
   His head is in a whirl,
Where stood the little bird just now
   There stands a little girl.

A Princess he can see she is,
   With a coronet of gold;
So the old man was a wizard, as
   The Little Bear had told.

RUPERT AND THE
MAGIC HAT

CHILDREN from every side then came,
    From the old man's spell set free;
No longer snakes or toads or frogs,
    But as they used to be.

"Rupert, come out! Come, Little Bear,"
    Called Robinson Crusoe;
"Here are the little ones. Show them.
    The way they have to go."

How gladly Rupert beckons them;
    They run to him, of course,
As he points the way to the Secret Door
    Beneath the Flying Horse.

RUPERT AND THE
MAGIC HAT

WHEN the last child had disappeared
    Down through that Secret Door
Crusoe follows, keeping still an eye
    On the old man and the Boar—

But not before he'd warned them that
    If on child or Little Bear
They played their tricks again, next time
    Their lives he would not spare.

Rupert, the children, too, who went
    Ahead wait anxiously,
Till Rupert cries: "Ah, here he is,"
    And Crusoe safe they see.

RUPERT AND THE
MAGIC HAT

HE takes the Princess by the hand;
    Rupert walks at his side.
The other children follow them
    To where Jack waits beside

The Magic Hat. Said Crusoe: "Now
    I think it's only right
That Jack and Rupert should be first
    To make the homeward flight."

RUPERT AND THE MAGIC HAT

THE Princess is to go with them;
   The Hat can carry three.
Crusoe puts Rupert in; then Jack.
   "Are you ready now?" said he.

"First you must take the Princess home,
   Then go without delay
To your own homes. Then bid the Hat
   Come back to me straightway."

RUPERT AND THE
MAGIC HAT

RUPERT spoke the words the Gnome had used:
   "Rise, Hat of Blunderbore."
To his joy at once it rises up
   And bears them from the shore.

The children wave while Crusoe calls:
   "Mind, Rupert, don't forget
To send it back. These little ones
   Have still to get home yet."

RUPERT AND THE
MAGIC HAT

SO swiftly flies the Magic Hat
    That ere much time had sped
The Princess bids them stop, for there
    She saw her home, she said.

They see a castle far below,
    And in its garden fair
They land the Princess, say farewell,
    And away once more in air.

RUPERT AND THE
MAGIC HAT

THEY fly above the countryside,
   Till seeing far below
His home, Jack calls: "That's where I live."
   So quickly down they go.

Soon as the Hat touched land Jack jumped;
   Glad is he to be there
At home and safe. He turns to say,
   Good-bye to Little Bear.

Then open comes the cottage door,
   And someone calls, "Oh, Jack,
I thought I'd ne'er see you again,
   And here you're safely back!"

RUPERT AND THE
MAGIC HAT

IT was Jack's brother. Then he stared,
  And said to Little Bear:
"I'm sure that I've seen you before;
  We must have met somewhere.

"Why, yes, I now remember well;
  'Twas the day I caught the Gnome
And was about to punish him
  For stealing Jack from home.

"You came and interfered. I said
  You would repent, you know."
"Yes," Rupert said, "I did full well;
  But, good-bye, I must go."

RUPERT AND THE
MAGIC HAT

RUPERT'S Mummy, weary, going home
    After searching everywhere
For him, and wondering where he'd gone,
    Anxious and full of care,

Sees then the strangest looking thing
    Come flying swift and fast.
A cheerful voice cries down to her:
    "Here I am, back at last."

Then Rupert lands. His Mother cries:
    "Good gracious me. What's that?"
"Oh, Mum, it's brought me home," said he.
    "It is the Magic Hat."

RUPERT AND THE MAGIC HAT

O'ERJOYED, she lifts him from the Hat.
    "Mum, wait a minute yet;
I've got to send it back," said he.
    "Crusoe bade me not forget."

Then turning to the Magic Hat
    He bids it rise once more;
"Go back. Return to Crusoe now,
    Magic Hat of Blunderbore."

"Oh, Mum," said he, "I've lots to tell
    Of that Hat and the Gnome."
"Come in," said she, "first have your tea;
    Glad am I you're safe home."

RUPERT AND THE MAGIC HAT

THE Magic Hat obeyed. It went straight back, across the sea
To Crusoe, where the children stood waiting expectantly.
Time after time it went and came till all were safely home
Free from the power of that old man, the Wild Boar and the
Gnome.
A Magic Hat will never act for grown-ups, as you know,
And so it could not carry home poor Robinson Crusoe.
He pondered as it rested there, beside him on the shore
Then made a bonfire, and he burned that Hat of Blunderbore
So that ne'er again could it be used by any wicked Gnomes
To tempt the children for a ride and steal them from their homes.
When this was done the captive Gnome by Crusoe was set free;
Without that Magic Hat, of course, he could not cross the sea.
And so the three, with Crusoe there, lived in great dread and fear,
Knowing that if they broke their word he'd make them pay full
dear.
So here's the end, and all may know that never, nevermore
Can harm to little children come through the Hat of Blunderbore.

THE END